FITZ AND THE FOOL
coloring book

CHARACTERS BY: ROBIN HOBB
ARTWORK BY: MANUEL PREITANO
PROJECT MANAGER: ERNST DABEL
BOOK DESIGN BY: LES DABEL
SPECIAL THANKS TO: SERENA MARENCO

FOLLOW US ONLINE:
WWW.DABELBROTHERS.COM

Twitter: @DabelBrothers
Facebook: facebook.com/dabelbrothers
Instagram: @DabelBrothers

DABEL BROTHERS:

Jay Gentry - CEO
Ernst Dabel - President
Les Dabel - V.P. Licensing
Derek Ruiz - Publisher
Patrick Victor - V.P. Sales

Wes Harris - V.P. Business Development
David Campiti - V.P. Creative & Development
Grant Alter - Editor-in-Chief
Dave Lanphear - Chief Creative Officer
Gladys Atwell - Marketing Director
Anthony Zicari: - Editor / Sr. Writer

FITZ & THEFOOL®: COLORING BOOK 2018.
Copyright ©2018 Margaret Lindholm Ogden. All rights reserved. Office of publication: 3330 Cobb Parkway N, Suite 324 #245, Acworth, GA 30101. Dabel Brothers Publishing and its logos are TM and © Dabel Brothers Publishing, LLC. **FITZ & THE FOOL®: COLORING BOOK** and all characters featured in this book and the distinctive names and likenesses thereof, and all related indicia are trademarks of Margaret Lindholm Ogden. All rights reserved. The characters in this publication are entirely fictional. No similarity between any of the names, characters, persons, and/or institutions in this book with those of any living or dead person or institutions is intended, and any such similarity which may exist is purely coincidental. No portion of this publication may be reproduced by any means without the written permission of the copyright holder except artwork used for review purposes.

Tips on how to color this Coloring Book:

Thank you for purchasing this Dabel Brothers Coloring Book.

It's one of many Coloring Books we currently have available from your favorite authors, book series, TV shows, movies, games, Musicians... the list goes on and will continue to grow as we add more amazing Coloring Books to our lineup.

If you enjoyed this Coloring Book please make sure to post your colored pages on our social media and leave us a review. We also encourage you to purchase a copy for your loved ones, as coloring is a great source of stress relief.

Make sure to visit our website **DabelBrothers.com** for news on upcoming titles and free goodies.

Yours Truly,

Dabel Brothers

1 Always test any markers before you start coloring, using the test page in the back of the book to see if the marker bleeds through or leaves a shadow.

2 If you are using a marker, paint or watercolor pencils, slip a piece of paper behind the page you are coloring to protect the pages behind from bleed through issues.

3 Have LOTS of fun coloring and always remember, coloring is twice as fun when you are coloring with others. So make sure you have plenty of copies of this book for you and your loved ones :)

 Motley and the Fool

 Verity

 Fitz, Nighteyes and the 'sleeping' dragons

 Molly

 Burrich

 Lord Golden

 Fitz and Chade

 The Crest of Buckkeep

 The Crest of Buckkeep 2

 Trehaug the "tree house city"

 Reyn and Malta

Verity and his dragon

 The Elderling City

Sea serpent

 Amber and Paragon

The Fool and Shrewd

 Fitz and the Queen

the Fool sings his gender song

 Patience and Lacey

Winterfest

 Kettricken with her ladies

TEST PAGE

Printed in Great Britain
by Amazon